WORD TRAVELERS

TRAVELERS

AND THE MISSING MEXICAN MOLÉ

THE
WORD
TRAVELERS
SERIES

The Taj Mahal Mystery

The Missing Mexican Molé

WORD TRAVELERS

AND THE **MISSING** MEXICAN MOLÉ

RAJ HALDAR

ILLUSTRATED BY **NEHA RAWAT**

sourcebooks
eXplore

Text and art copyright © 2022 by Raj Haldar
Cover and internal design © 2022 by Sourcebooks
Cover design by Maryn Arreguín/Sourcebooks
Internal design by Jillian Rahn/Sourcebooks
Cover and internal illustrations by Neha Rawat

Published by Sourcebooks eXplore, an imprint of Sourcebooks Kids
P.O. Box 4410, Naperville, Illinois 60567–4410
(630) 961-3900
sourcebookskids.com

Cataloging-in-Publication Data is on file with the Library of Congress.

Source of Production: Sheridan Books, Chelsea, MI, United States
Date of Production: November 2021
Run Number: 5023686

Printed and bound in the United States of America.
SB 10 9 8 7 6 5 4 3 2 1

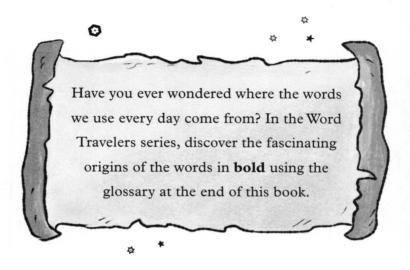

Have you ever wondered where the words we use every day come from? In the Word Travelers series, discover the fascinating origins of the words in **bold** using the glossary at the end of this book.

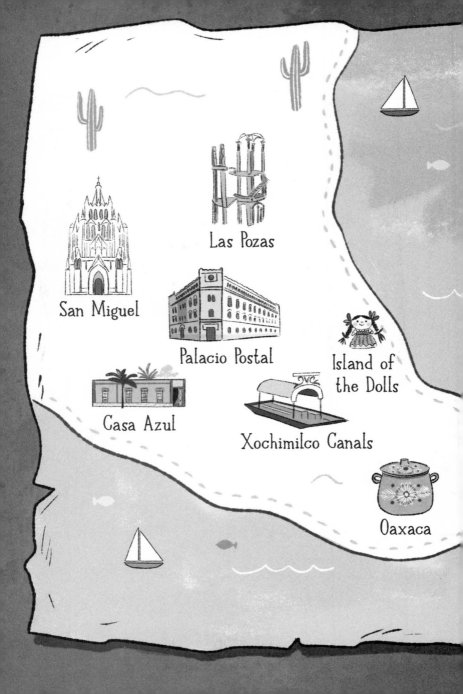

Las Pozas

San Miguel

Palacio Postal

Island of
the Dolls

Casa Azul

Xochimilco Canals

Oaxaca

Welcome to **Mexico**

Chichén Itzá

Lacandon Jungle

1

COSTUME CONFIDENTIAL

"Boo!" MJ's mom peeked into her bedroom wearing a pointy black hat, "Do you need help with your costume, Molly-Jean?"

Digging through an old trunk, MJ finally found her beat-up leather bomber jacket. "Now where are those aviator pins that Eddie got me for my birthday last year?"

MJ's mom let out a sigh as she turned around to head back downstairs. "Let me guess, you're dressing up as Amelia Earhart...*again*."

MJ smiled to herself. Ever since she read a biography of the great Amelia Earhart, MJ had been positively obsessed. Amelia was one of her all-time heroes, and every Halloween meant dressing up as the famous woman pilot.

"Eddie and his parents are going to be here any minute now!" MJ's mom called out from the bottom of the stairs.

Just then, the doorbell rang. Before her mom could shout at her again, MJ yelled down, "I'm coming! Just a sec!"

After MJ completed her costume, she bounded down the stairs. She could hear her best friend, Eddie, doing a funny impression. "Look-see, I'm a gumshoe, but that doesn't mean there's gum on my shoes!" he joked, talking from the side of his mouth. He was dressed in a long brown trench coat, probably from his dad's closet. On his head, Eddie wore a fedora hat with a wide brim. In his left hand, MJ spied a magnifying glass.

"You're a detective!" MJ guessed as she reached the bottom of the stairs.

"You got it, Mac!" Eddie responded, staying totally in character. "Now, let's quit the horsing around and get this Halloween party started."

2

THE HALLOWEEN PARTY

Eddie and MJ's families loved their little traditions, and Halloween was no exception. Each year, MJ's mom and dad invited Eddie's parents over for a Halloween party. Everyone got into the spirit. MJ's mom set up a jack-o-lantern carving station in the kitchen. And they always ordered pizza for dinner.

Eddie's dad was already goofing around doing

the "Monster Mash" dance, making everyone laugh. "Happy All Hallows' Eve, everyone!" bellowed Eddie's dad as he plopped down on the sofa, out of breath from his kooky dance.

"You mean Halloween?" asked MJ.

"Oh no, little buddy," he replied, shaking his head. "Halloween is a shortened way of saying All Hallows' Eve. That's what they called it way back in the Middle Ages in Scotland, where the tradition started."

MJ sounded it out. "All Hallows' Eve. Hall—ow—e'en. *Whoa!*"

After carving their pump-kins, the friends ate dinner. MJ felt like she had finished her one-and-a-half slices of pizza hours ago. Now, she was getting impatient with Eddie, who was taking forever to eat as usual. "Since when did you start eating your pizza backward, Eddie?" she asked, rolling her eyes.

"I like to get the crust out of the way first so I can enjoy all this cheesy goodness!" Eddie replied as he pulled the slice away, stretching a string of cheese the length of his arm with it. MJ laughed. With one gigantic bite, Eddie finished the last of his dinner and looked up from his plate. "C'mon, let's go! It's time to…"

"Treat or trick!" they shouted together.

Two years ago, MJ and Eddie had decided to switch the order of the words when MJ learned that "trick" in trick-or-treat meant a prank that children played on grown-ups who didn't hand out candy. "No one does the trick part anymore, so why should it go first?" she always said.

"It's getting dark out there. You kids better get moving!" said MJ's mom as she opened the front

door. With that, they fixed up their costumes and dashed out into the crisp fall night.

There were exactly thirteen houses on Magnolia Street, where Eddie and MJ lived.

The two costumed friends made their way up the street, stopping at every single house. By the time they reached the end of the street, the bags they used to collect their treats were almost full. There was only one house left. All the way at the top of Magnolia Street was number thirteen, the oldest house on the block.

"We can just skip number thirteen," Eddie said nervously. "We've already got lots of candy..."

Every Halloween, the rumors would spread. The neighborhood kids whispered that the elderly lady, Mrs. Calavera, who lived with her daughter at the old house at the end of the street would cast a spell on you if you went trick-or-treating there.

Suddenly, a bolt of lightning lit up the night sky. The wind picked up, clattering the shutters of the old house. It started to rain, and Eddie felt more than ever that 13 Magnolia Street was something straight out of a haunted house movie.

"Thirteen is an unlucky number—" Eddie started.

"Don't tell me you have triskaidekaphobia, Eddie!" said MJ, shaking her head.

"I feel just fine, thank you," replied Eddie, touching the back of his hand to his forehead.

"No, silly! It's a big word for when people are scared of the number thirteen. But, in some countries, thirteen is actually a lucky number!" MJ said. "Now, let's go."

MJ tugged her friend by his trench coat, and the two made their way toward the rickety front door.

"I...I don't think anyone's home, MJ," Eddie whispered, as he stepped backward away from the old house.

"Not so fast," said MJ. She reached up on her tippy-toes and pressed the doorbell.

Ding-dong!

Slowly, the front door creaked open. Eddie could barely make out the shadow of a woman towering above them. At her feet, a black cat scurried out into the yard.

"Gato!" the lady screeched. Stepping into the light, Eddie and MJ finally got a good look at the woman. It was Mrs. Calavera's grown-up daughter, Elena.

"Hola, kids," she said, looking down at Eddie and MJ.

"Treat or trick, Ms. Elena!" MJ said excitedly. She knew better than to believe all those silly rumors about the Calaveras.

Ms. Elena looked down with a great big smile. "I almost forgot it was Halloween since all the other kids have stopped coming to our house."

"Where's your mom, Mrs. Calavera?" asked MJ.

"*Dios mío!* You didn't hear?" replied Ms. Elena with a frown. "My mother passed away just a few months ago." Ms. Elena's eyes got watery, and a teardrop rolled down her cheek.

"I'm so sorry," MJ said.

"Thank you, but it's okay. She was one hundred five years old and had a long, wonderful life," Ms. Elena said. She smiled at the trick-or-treaters just as the rain let up, and the clouds gave way to a glowing full moon. "Actually, it makes me very happy that you came here, because my mother loved to hand out candy on Halloween," she remembered. "Let me see. I know Mother always kept some goodies in the drawer right here." Ms. Elena turned around, rooting through an old cabinet in the front room of the house. "Aha! Here we are," she said, dropping a treat into MJ's bag. Ms. Elena looked down and winked at Eddie and MJ. "Mother must have known you'd be coming, because she left a big candy for you to share. Happy Halloween!"

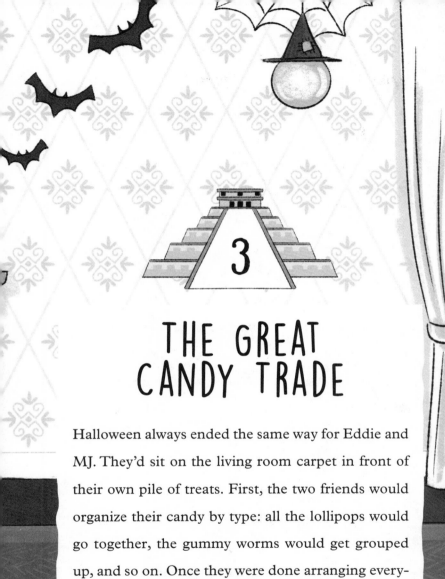

3

THE GREAT CANDY TRADE

Halloween always ended the same way for Eddie and MJ. They'd sit on the living room carpet in front of their own pile of treats. First, the two friends would organize their candy by type: all the lollipops would go together, the gummy worms would get grouped up, and so on. Once they were done arranging everything, the Great Candy Trade would begin!

"I'll give you three packs of candy corn for that big box of watermelon bubble gum," MJ said.

"Sold!" Eddie replied.

Just as they were finishing their last trade, Eddie noticed something colorful laying on the carpet a few feet away. "That wasn't there before, was it?"

MJ knelt and got a closer look. "It's the candy bar Ms. Elena gave us from her mother, Mrs. Calavera. It must've tumbled away when we dumped our treats onto the floor."

"That doesn't look like any of the usual candy bars," Eddie said as he walked over to MJ. The wrapper had a striking pattern of colorful blue, orange, and yellow triangles. MJ carefully opened the outer wrapper, revealing a golden foil inside.

"This is the most beautiful candy bar I've ever seen!" said MJ.

Not able to wait any longer, Eddie grabbed the curious candy from MJ and started unwrapping the

16

golden foil. Inside was a chocolate bar with something strange pressed onto it: *CHOCOLATL*.

"What the heck?" said Eddie. "This must be some kind of mistake. Chocolate ends with an E, not an L."

"I don't know, Eddie," MJ said, turning the candy over in her hands. "Who would make such a gorgeous candy bar and then forgot how to spell chocolate? There must be something more to it."

The two kids looked at each other with a knowing glance. "We need the AEB!"

The Awesome Enchanted Book—or AEB as they called it for short—was a special kind of dictionary that explained where all the words in the English language come from. Not only that, the AEB also had magical powers!

In a flash, Eddie and MJ raced across the living room past their parents and up the stairs to MJ's bedroom. MJ reached under her bed, where they had stored it for safekeeping, and pulled out the big old book.

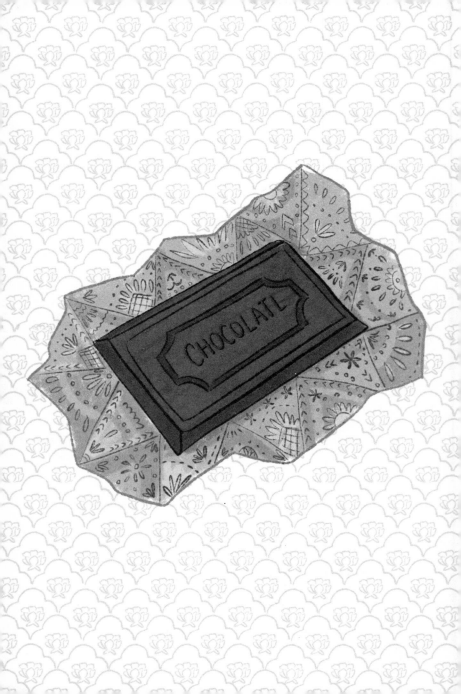

"Let's start with the letter C. For **chocolate**!" Eddie exclaimed.

The AEB was organized just like an ordinary dictionary, with all the words in alphabetical order. They found the section for words that start with the letter C.

"Chocolate sounds like it's French or something," MJ said to herself as she ran her fingers across the pages. "If we can just find it here. Champion... chimpanzee..."

"There!" shouted Eddie, pointing to the opposite page.

MJ read the entry from the AEB aloud. "From a word used by the ancient Aztecs, *chocolatl*..."

"It ends in an L! Like it says on the candy bar!" Eddie interrupted.

"It was originally prepared as a drink; in the Nahuatl language used by the Aztecs, the word *at-l* means hot water," MJ continued.

"The ancient Aztecs drank hot chocolate just like

us," Eddie whispered. "Where in the world did the Aztecs live again?" he wondered. "I know we learned about this in school, but I can't remember…"

At that very moment, the AEB began floating above their heads, spinning faster and faster, until the room was filled with a swirling haze of smoke, and—*poof!*

4

THE BIG SWEET

"Eddie!" MJ called out. A noisy ceiling fan above helped clear away the smoke that filled the room. She could see her best friend sitting nearby on an old wooden desk. "Where in the world are we?" she gasped.

Eddie kicked his feet up on the desk. "I couldn't tell ya, Mac," he replied, noticing that he still had his private eye costume on. Looking around, Eddie saw a shabby office with some beat-up filing cabinets in the corner. "But it does suit me pretty good."

At the far end of the room, they saw a large door with a frosted glass window. "Look!" MJ said. "There's something written on the door."

"I don't know, MJ," shrugged Eddie. "Looks like a bunch of gobbledygook to me."

MJ studied the symbols on the window, scratching her head. Suddenly, it came to her. "How could we be so foolish? The letters are written backward because the sign is meant to be read from the outside."

"You're right!" Eddie exclaimed, already starting to work out the words. "Oficina de…"

MJ interrupted. "That means *office* in Spanish! I remember it from a sign in my doctor's waiting room back home!"

Eddie's eyes got wide as it dawned on him. "We're in a detective's office!" he shouted.

"But it's in Spanish. Does that mean we're in Spain?" MJ added quizzically.

Just then, Eddie and MJ heard the sound of music wafting in through a window in the corner of the room. Running over to get a better look, MJ saw a group of men on the street below playing trumpets, violins, and guitars. "Wowza!" exclaimed MJ.

"Holy **guacamole**!" Eddie blurted out. "They look like musicians from when we learned about Cinco de Mayo at school! Don't you remember our celebration?"

"That's right," said MJ. "On the the fifth of May every year, we celebrate the food, music, and all of the other awesome stuff we get from…"

"The country that has the most Spanish-speaking people in the whole world," added Eddie, tipping his detective hat and smiling.

"We're in Mexico!" they said at exactly the same time.

Suddenly, the door swung open. A girl who was just a few years older than Eddie and MJ burst into the office. She had a worried look on her face. "My family needs your help, Señor Detective," she said.

"Slow down! You've got it all wrong," said

Eddie. "I'm not actually a detective. I just happen to be inside a detective's office, wearing a detective's outfit..." Eddie trailed off, realizing how ridiculous he sounded.

"This is no time to be humble, señor!" pleaded the girl.

The two friends looked at each other and decided right there and then to take the case.

"Eddie and Molly-Jean Detective Agency, at your service, ma'am," Eddie said, with the drawl of one of those movie investigators.

"Oh, gracias!" the girl said, letting out a sigh of relief. "My name is Rosa. I came here because my family's restaurant is in big trouble."

"What happened?" MJ asked.

"You see, each year thousands of people come from all around to our little town of San Miguel to celebrate Día de los Muertos, the Day of the Dead."

"Sounds spooky!" said Eddie.

MJ shook her head and sighed. "Don't you remember, Eddie? Día de los Muertos is the holiday that people celebrate here in Mexico at the beginning of November."

"Yes," Rosa continued. "It takes place around the same time as Halloween, but we have our own customs and traditions. Día de los Muertos is a joyful holiday where we celebrate the memory of our ancestors who have died by telling funny stories about them and enjoying their favorite foods. On the final night of celebrations, everyone goes to the big graveyard here in San Miguel for a gigantic party with music and tasty treats for all. And that's the problem…"

"Give us the scoop, Rosa," Eddie said.

"Well, my family restaurant is famous for making a special dish called **molé**," explained Rosa. "The trouble is, Abuelita, my grandmother, is the only one who knows the secret recipe, and she's gone missing!"

"Oh no!" MJ shouted.

Rosa sighed. "If we don't find Abuelita soon, we won't have the molé ready in time for the big party, and the family restaurant could go out of business for good."

"We don't have a second to lose," replied Eddie. "We have to find Abuelita now!"

MJ grabbed the Awesome Enchanted Book from the desk, and the three friends darted out of the detective's office.

5

SAN MIGUEL

Stepping out onto the cobblestone streets of San Miguel, Eddie and MJ couldn't believe their eyes. The town looked like something out of a fairy tale. Every house lining the street was painted a different color of the rainbow. The townspeople were buzzing about in the warm afternoon sun, preparing for the Día de los Muertos celebration the following evening.

LA FAMILIA

"Come this way." Rosa motioned for the kids to follow her down a narrow alleyway. Suddenly, the alley opened up into a huge **plaza**.

"Many towns in Mexico have an open area like this where people can gather and spend time."

"Ooh!" Eddie said, stopping for a moment to take in the tree-lined square, dotted with park benches.

When they finally got to the big church at the far end of the plaza, Rosa pointed down another small cobblestone alley. "This way. We're almost there!"

Halfway down the street, MJ and Eddie knew they had arrived at the restaurant. Looking at the battered old sign hanging above the building, Eddie read the name out loud. "La Familia... The Family!"

"Yes!" exclaimed Rosa. "The perfect name for

our restaurant, since everyone in our family has worked here for generations." Through the window, they saw a burly man with a gray mustache rolling out dough. "That's my father, Nacho!"

"Like the chips?" Eddie blurted out.

Rosa laughed. "Nacho is a common nickname for boys with the name Ignacio. The story goes that the person who came up with the recipe for nacho chips was named Ignacio."

Nacho wiped the flour from his hands onto his

apron and waved to MJ and Eddie. "Hola! You must be the detectives from the agency," he said, letting out a sigh of relief. "Thank you so much for coming here! Why don't you take a look inside our apartment upstairs? That's where Abuelita was last seen before she disappeared."

Eddie and MJ raced up the wooden stairs to the apartment above the restaurant. "Welcome to our humble abode," Rosa said, showing the detective duo into her home.

Through the entryway, MJ could see the kitchen, living room, and three bedrooms down the back hallway. "It has everything we need, plus, it makes getting to work a **breeze**!"

"Hey, what's this?" Eddie asked, pointing toward a little table in the living room. It was chock full of framed photos surrounded by colorful orange and yellow flowers.

"That's our ofrenda," Rosa said.

"No, I didn't mean to offend you!" Eddie replied.

Rosa laughed, saying the Spanish word more slowly. "It's our *o-frend-a*. For Día de los Muertos, families make a small altar in their homes to celebrate their ancestors. We fill it with old photos of our loved ones and decorate it with colorful flowers and calaveras. Those are the little candy skulls made of sugar."

MJ walked over to the ofrenda to get a closer look. A black-and-white photo with torn edges caught her eye. It was a picture of two girls on a mountain trail.

"That's Abuelita and her sister, Maria, in the mountain village they grew up in," Rosa replied. "Where are you, Abuelita?"

"Don't worry, Rosa," MJ said. "We're going to find her if it's the last thing we do!"

"We just need a lead…some kind of clue," Eddie said under his breath.

Just then, there was a knock at the front door.

"That must be the mailman," Rosa said. A stack of envelopes slid under the door.

Rosa's eyes fell on a small envelope with Abuelita's

handwriting on it. "*Dios mío!* Oh my goodness! Abuelita wrote this letter to her sister, who still lives back in the old village. But the address is all smudged, so the postman returned it!"

She opened the envelope, and her smile quickly turned into a frown. Rosa showed the letter to her friends.

> The **barracuda** is greedy,
> A mole needs feeding.
> Hurry, be speedy,
> At the palace, come meet me!

"It's just a bunch of nonsense," she sighed. "Abuelita has gotten a little kooky in her old age."

"**Barracuda**," said MJ, looking at Eddie. "That's a killer fish, right?"

"This sounds like a job for the AEB," Eddie replied, grabbing the book from MJ. "Let's see... Here we go," he pointed at the entry for the word *barracuda*. "It comes from a Spanish word that means *overlapping teeth*!"

"A snaggletooth sea dweller," said MJ with a scowl on her face. "That doesn't get us anywhere."

"Wait," Rosa whispered, as she walked toward the apartment window and opened the blinds. "I know someone with a whole mouthful of overlapping teeth. It's Groucho Gary," she said, pointing down at a sign that read Groucho Gary's **Barbecue**. "He just opened a shiny new restaurant across the street from La Familia, and he's been trying to take away our customers since day one."

Looking at the second line of the letter, MJ realized something. "This doesn't mean mole like the animal," she said, looking at Eddie. "Abuelita is tricky! She left the accent off the word, which changes the meaning completely." MJ said, looking up at Rosa. "Abuelita is talking about your family's molé recipe!"

"The barracuda is greedy, a molé needs feeding,"

Eddie whispered to himself. "Groucho Gary is after your family's molé recipe," he exclaimed.

"At the palace, come meet me," said Rosa, reading the last line of the letter. "What kind of palace could Abuelita be talking about?"

Eddie inspected the envelope with his detective's magnifying glass. "Look at the postmark stamped on here!"

"Of course!" said Rosa. "The Palacio Post Office in Mexico City, our country's capital. Abuelita must be on her way there now, but she has no idea that the letter never got to her sister..."

"We have to get there fast and let Abuelita know that Maria never got the message to meet her," MJ said.

Eddie sailed out the door, long trench coat flapping behind him. "Let's go," he insisted. "I mean, **vamoose!**"

In an instant, they were back out on the street. Rosa whistled loudly to get the attention of a taxi driver waiting on the corner. "To the Palacio Post Office," she exclaimed. **"Pronto!"**

NO ORDINARY
POST OFFICE

"Right here is fine," said Rosa, as their bright pink
taxi screeched to a halt.

"Muchas gracias!" they all exclaimed, thanking
the driver as they opened the door and bounced out
of the taxi.

MJ stared up at the beautiful old building in
front of them. "I think you've got something mixed

up, Rosa," she said. "We're supposed to be looking for a *post office*."

Rosa laughed. "This is no ordinary post office," she said as she pulled open the two massive doors.

"It's dazzling," MJ said. From either side of the lobby, two huge sets of stairs shot up from the marble floor, meeting at a landing that seemed to float in the center of the grand old building. Looking up, Eddie could see that the ceiling of the Palacio Post Office was made entirely of glass, drenching the whole place in sunlight.

"This post office is a palace, all right!" Eddie said as the trio walked into the center of the busy lobby. "I can't believe people come to a place like this just to send letters and buy stamps."

"How will we ever find Abuelita in such a busy place?" MJ sighed. There were several lines snaking around the lobby, and a group of tourists taking pictures while listening to a tour guide.

MJ overheard the tour guide speak. "Once you've

finished taking photos, feel free to visit the popcorn seller just to your left," he said. "In fact, the popped corn snack that is enjoyed in movie theaters all over the world was first invented here in Mexico!"

"Amigos," Rosa whispered to Eddie and MJ. "Abuelita loves popcorn! She would never pass up the chance to have a handful of it."

"Maybe the popcorn seller has seen Abuelita?" Eddie guessed.

In a flash, the three friends ran over to the popcorn seller. "Señor, have you seen my abuelita? She's a little old lady who wears her dark black hair in a ponytail. I'm sure she stopped for some popcorn this morning!"

"I do seem to remember someone fitting that description coming to my illustrious stand

43

not too long ago," the man said, wiping popcorn butter from his hands. "Curious..." he started.

"What is it?" cried MJ.

"Yes," the popcorn seller said. "I remember now! She was thrilled to have a taste of my world-famous popcorn, but something happened." The man looked around and continued in a hushed tone. "I think something startled her, because she rushed off without her snack."

"Did she say where she was going?" Eddie asked.

The nice man thought for a moment. "I think she was headed toward the mailroom," he said. "It's just up those stairs." He motioned with his popcorn scoop. They looked up and saw a door at the landing of the second-floor balcony.

"Thanks, señor! We'd better scram," Eddie said, sounding just like one of those movie detectives. With that, the kids scrambled up the grand staircase of Palacio Post Office.

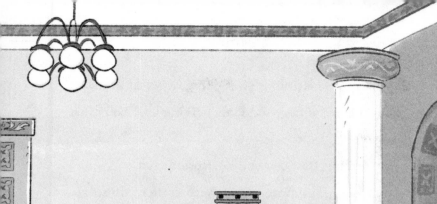

THE MAILROOM

Looking around the mailroom, Eddie saw what looked like a hundred little lockers behind a long counter.

"I remember Abuelita bringing me here when I was a small girl," Rosa remembered. "She rented one of these mailboxes."

Standing at the counter was a tall man with a long, gray beard and a pencil behind his ear. "Can

I help you?" he muttered, looking down at the kids. "Oh!" he exclaimed, suddenly perking up. "You must be Rosa."

"Yes, but how did you—" Rosa began.

"Your grandmother was here earlier," the man interrupted. "Abuelita thought you might come looking for her, so she asked me to give you this." The clerk slid Rosa a scrap of paper with some words scrawled on it.

Here is the key:
Six numbers, open sesame!
Siesta, Siesta,
Once and for all.
*Tan Galan, **Buckaroo!***

"It's all Greek to me!" said MJ with a shrug.

"Not so fast," whispered Rosa. "That last English word,

buckaroo. It came to your English language from our Spanish word, *vaquero*, which means 'cowboy.'"

"They do sound alike," said Eddie.

"Okay, so working backward," MJ began. "*Tan Galan*—that sure sounds like Spanish."

"Yes," Rosa replied. "It means 'so gallant.' I'm not sure how that helps us."

"Gallant means 'polite' or 'gracious,'" Eddie offered.

"A polite cowboy," muttered MJ.

Suddenly, Eddie's eyes lit up. His best friend MJ knew that expression very well. "You're onto something, aren't you, Eddie?" she asked.

"Boy, am I glad I was obsessed with cowboy movies in second grade," Eddie said. "MJ, in all the old Westerns they have a special name for those big, old cowboy hats! They call them *ten-gallon hats*."

"Maybe because they're so big they could fit ten gallons of water?" MJ suggested as she whipped open the AEB. "Here we go," she said, pointing to the entry for **ten-gallon hat**.

"A big cowboy hat with a large brim. It comes from the Spanish phrase *tan galan*, which means 'very gallant.' Eddie, you're a genius!"

"So, the code probably ends with the number ten," said Rosa, piecing the clues together.

"Right. But according to Abuelita's clue, the combination to the lockbox has a total of six numbers," replied MJ as she scanned the scrap of paper again. "My parents use the word *siesta* all the time. It's an afternoon nap, isn't it?"

Rosa nodded.

Eddie grabbed the AEB from MJ. "Found it!" he exclaimed. "You two are not going to believe this," Eddie continued. "The Spanish word *siesta*, which means 'afternoon nap,' was originally meant to be taken on the *sixth* hour after sunrise."

Just then, Rosa noticed the post office clerk

leaning over the counter listening in, so she lowered her voice. "The number six," she whispered.

"Siesta, siesta! There's two of them in the clue," Eddie noticed. "The code begins with two sixes."

Rosa looked down at the paper once more. "Now we just need the middle two numbers."

"Don't worry! I've already got that figured out," said MJ, beaming with pride. "I taught myself to count to one hundred in Spanish this year, and I noticed something interesting about the number eleven."

Eddie began counting on his fingers, "Eight is ocho, nine is nueve, ten is diez…"

"Once!" Rosa cried out.

"Exactly," said MJ. "Abuelita is using the English word *once* in her clue, but it's also the same word for the number eleven in Spanish."

"Pronounced like *own-say!*" Eddie said.

Huddling up in front of Abuelita's lockbox, Rosa entered the combination, 6-6-1-1-1-0, and held her

breath. All of a sudden there was a click, and the door to the small lockbox swung open.

"We did it!" MJ shouted. "There's money inside!"

Rosa pulled out a crisp new bill. "This is our new 500-peso note," she said. "It has a portrait of the famous Mexican artist Frida Kahlo on the front of it," Rosa continued. "She's my hero!"

"There's something written on the back," Eddie said. Rosa flipped over the bill, instantly recognizing Abuelita's handwriting. She read aloud:

*A **burrito***
In a Blue House
Holds a special key.
***Tornado** to the left,*
And set the next clue free.

Just then, the post office clerk pulled off his fake beard and smiled, exposing a mouthful of uneven teeth. "Of course! The Blue House is Casa Azul, the home of Frida Kahlo," he sneered as he snatched the bill from the kids and ran off.

For a moment, MJ, Eddie, and Rosa stood there stunned. "Did…did you see his teeth?" Rosa asked.

"That was Groucho Gary, wasn't it?" MJ replied furiously. "He disguised himself as the clerk so that he could get the next clue from us!"

"Hurry!" Rosa exclaimed. "There's no time to be upset. We have to get to Frida Kahlo's Blue House, *La Casa Azul.*"

8

THE BLUEST
BLUE HOUSE

The kids made it from one end of Mexico City to another in record time, taking a bus to a train to yet another bus, and then walking for more than twenty minutes! On the way, Rosa told Eddie and MJ all about her hero—the painter Frida Kahlo. She was Mexico's most famous artist, best known for making beautiful portraits of herself. She grew up in and lived most of her life at Casa Azul. After she died, the house was turned into a museum where children and adults could visit to see where the artist had lived and worked.

As Eddie turned the corner onto a tree-lined street, he knew they had finally arrived. "No wonder they call it Casa Azul," he said excitedly. "This

must be the bluest blue house in the history of blue houses!"

The last tour of the home was just finishing up as they slipped in. "Almost everyone's gone for the day," MJ said.

"Better for us," said Rosa, smiling at her friends.

Inside the gates of the house was a beautiful

57

garden with all sorts of tropical plants and flowers. "This place is amazing!" said Eddie. Looking around, he suddenly spied Groucho Gary through a window in the house. "Look," he whispered, pointing into the home's kitchen.

"A burrito in a blue house," MJ whispered, remembering what Abuelita wrote on the 500-peso bill. "If Groucho Gary finds the burrito first, he's sure to get to the molé recipe before we do."

As Gary frantically searched the kitchen inside, Rosa had another idea. "Maybe a burrito isn't what we think it is."

"What do you mean?" said Eddie. "We *are* talking about those amazing tortillas stuffed with meat, beans, cheese, and veggies, like they have at our school cafeteria, right?" he asked.

"Well, yes," Rosa replied. "But do you know where the word **burrito** comes from?"

Before Rosa could answer her own question, MJ whipped out the AEB in a flash. "Here it is," she said. "*Burrito* is the Spanish word for…" Suddenly, MJ started laughing uncontrollably. She chortled so hard that she could hardly catch her breath.

"Have you lost your marbles?!" Eddie exclaimed. "What is it?"

MJ tried getting it together, but the giggles kept coming. Finally, she got the words out. "*Burrito* is a Spanish word for a baby donkey!"

"You're right," Rosa explained. "The word for a grown-up donkey is *burro*, and anything with *ito* on the end is 'baby' in Spanish. It's a way of showing affection!"

"Burr-ito." MJ sounded the word out to herself. As soon as the word came out of her mouth, MJ's eyes landed on something incredible. Hanging from the orange tree in the courtyard of Casa Azul was a **piñata**. She always asked her mom for a piñata on her birthday and loved to take turns hitting the colorful decoration until it broke and the candy showered down on her and her friends. "The piñata is in the shape of a baby donkey," MJ whispered.

As dusk fell, the kids tiptoed across the garden of Casa Azul toward the orange tree. "A burrito in a Blue House holds a special key..." Eddie whispered Abuelita's clue. "We have to get whatever's inside that burrito." He picked up a branch off the ground and smiled at Rosa and MJ. Winding up the tree branch like a baseball bat, Eddie took a swing.

Whiff!

He wasn't tall enough to reach the piñata at all.

"Let me try," suggested Rosa. She was at least a few inches taller than MJ and Eddie. "Uno, dos, tres..." Rosa counted off, letting loose a powerful swing. With a pop, the piñata exploded, raining down candy onto the grass below.

Among the colorful candies, MJ spotted something glimmering on the ground. "A key!" she whispered.

Abuelita, you are brilliant, Rosa thought to herself as she picked up the brass key.

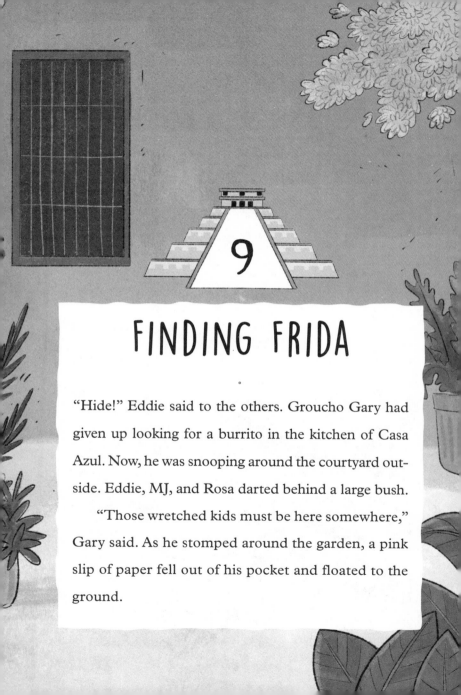

9

FINDING FRIDA

"Hide!" Eddie said to the others. Groucho Gary had given up looking for a burrito in the kitchen of Casa Azul. Now, he was snooping around the courtyard outside. Eddie, MJ, and Rosa darted behind a large bush.

"Those wretched kids must be here somewhere," Gary said. As he stomped around the garden, a pink slip of paper fell out of his pocket and floated to the ground.

MJ reached out from the bushes and picked it up. "It's the 500-peso note," she whispered. Turning it over, she squinted to read the second part of the message again:

Tornado to the left,
and set the next clue free.

MJ threw the AEB to Eddie.

Faster than he ever had before, Eddie found the entry for **tornado** and began to read. "Tornado comes from the Spanish word, *tornar*, which means 'to turn.'"

At once, the three kids turned to their left. Amazingly, they noticed a single bedroom with its lights on inside Casa Azul.

"That light wasn't on before," Eddie said excitedly. "We've gotta get up to that room."

As soon as the coast was clear, the trio left their hiding spot in the bushes and began to make their way over to the back entrance of Casa Azul. Rosa made sure that no one saw as they slipped into the house.

In total darkness, MJ, Eddie, and Rosa scampered up the back stairs. When they reached the top, they were met with a closed door. "This must be Frida Kahlo's famous bedroom where she liked to paint," Rosa said to the others.

Eddie gingerly tried the doorknob. "It's locked," he said. Instantly, Rosa pulled out the key they found inside the piñata and handed it to him. Eddie slid the brass key into the keyhole and turned the knob. Then, without warning, the door creaked open as if it had a mind of its own.

"Whoa," Eddie said under his breath.

They found themselves in a cozy bedroom. The room was filled with stunning artifacts and trinkets from all over Mexico. In the far corner, MJ spied a woman seated in a chair with a paintbrush in her hand.

The beautiful woman turned around, revealing a hazy glow all around her "Welcome children," she said in a ghostly voice. "I'm Frida Kahlo."

Frida stood up from her painting easel and began slowly walking toward the trio. It wasn't scary, though. Frida smiled as she spoke again, "Thank you for coming here to my home."

Eddie looked at the half-finished canvas on the

easel. It was a colorful painting of some boats float-ing down a canal. As he was studying the artwork, Frida continued, "Everyone knows me for my self-portraits—the paintings of myself. But, most of all I want to show the beauty of Mexico and its people, especially the ancient cultures like the Aztecs..."

"Yes! Before people from Spain ever visited our country, Mexico was already such an amazing place," Rosa replied. "The ancient Aztecs and Mayans and Olmecs gave the world so many things: food, art, and words too. But so much of it has already vanished!"

"You're right, Rosa," Frida said softly. "Now, you must do your best to make sure that Abuelita's molé recipe doesn't disappear too."

"You know Abuelita?" asked Rosa, eyes wide with amazement.

Frida laughed softly. "Just look at my painting to discover where your adventure will take you next." The artist turned back and looked at her easel. "Go now to the canals of Xochimilco."

"Zo-chi-who?!" Eddie exclaimed.

Rosa turned to her friends and repeated the name slowly so they would remember it. "Zo-chi-mil-co. In Mexico, words that start with the letter X can often make a Z sound or even an H sound. It comes from Nahuatl, the language of the ancient Aztecs," she explained. "Xochimilco isn't far from here," she continued. "For hundreds of years, visitors have enjoyed taking boats along the canals there."

"Wow!" MJ exclaimed.

"When you get to Xochimilco, don't forget to find *La Isla de las Muñecas,* the Island of the Dolls," added Frida. "And don't be scared. Abuelita left something very special there for you to find."

"What is it?" Rosa whispered.

"A doll, of course. Your grandmother's most treasured toy from when she was a child," Frida replied. With that, the famous Frida Kahlo faded away and vanished from sight.

CAPTAIN OF THE CANAL

The morning sun was shining bright by the time Eddie, MJ, and Rosa reached Xochimilco. There were already several long, multicolored boats floating along the canals. In each boat, MJ saw groups of friends and families chatting, eating snacks, and enjoying themselves. Rosa bought delicious corn on the cob for the whole gang.

"Welcome to Xochimilco!" shouted one of the boat operators, seeing the three kids standing at the dock. The man threw Eddie a rope. "Pull me a bit closer so you can jump aboard," he said with a smile. Rosa carefully boarded the craft, then extended her hand to help Eddie and MJ. "I'm Ernesto," the man introduced himself. "It's your lucky day, because my boat here is the fastest in all of Xochimilco!"

The musicians from a neighboring boat serenaded everyone in earshot. For a second, MJ felt like she was on one of her family vacations where she didn't have a care in the world. Then, suddenly something caught her eye.

"Eddie, is that Groucho Gary?" MJ nudged her friend.

"Where?!" Eddie replied, spitting a mouthful of corn out of his mouth in the process.

"On the next boat," said Rosa, who was listening in. "He's playing guitar in the band. The man in the big sombrero." Eddie looked over and spotted a man in a gigantic Mexican hat with a guitar in his hand. Opening his mouth wide to sing, the man exposed his mouthful of crooked teeth.

"Groucho Gary's singing voice is awful!" Eddie said, putting his hands over his ears dramatically.

"Stop!" shouted MJ. But it was too late. Groucho Gary had already noticed them.

"You kids think you're so clever, but I'm hot on your trail!" Gary hollered across the boats.

"Ernesto, we gotta go!" said Eddie, looking back at the boat captain. Ernesto nodded and pulled on the rip cord of his little engine. The deafening sound of the motor drowned out all the chatter and music from the canal as the boat started picking up speed.

"Buckle up!" said Ernesto, as he expertly weaved his craft around the other boats in the canal.

MJ looked back and saw that Groucho Gary's boat wasn't far behind. "He's getting closer!" she warned.

"Look out!" Rosa cried, pointing ahead in the distance at an oncoming boat.

Ernesto yanked the ship's wheel to the left. MJ and Eddie grabbed on tight as their boat tilted sideways. "I think I might lose my lunch!" Eddie said. Suddenly, Ernesto jerked the wheel in the other direction, steadying the craft. They had avoided the oncoming boat, but only by a hair.

MJ wiped a bead of sweat from her forehead. "Phew! That was close!"

"We're not in the clear yet," replied Eddie. Groucho Gary was right on their tail. "Hold my corn!" said Ernesto, handing his half-eaten cob to MJ. "No one knows the canals of Xochimilco like I do."

The boat captain cranked up the engine,

crisscrossing the maze of canals. Left, then, right. Another quick left.

"I'm starting to get dizzy," MJ whispered, grabbing on to the nearest railing.

Ernesto looked back and saw Groucho Gary fading into the distance. "Ha! I told you kids, there's no match for me on these canals!"

"Look out!" Eddie yelled suddenly. There was a broken-down boat up ahead.

"The canal is too narrow here to go around it," cried MJ as they barreled forward.

Ernesto looked back at MJ and said "Hold the wheel!"

"Me?!" she said.

"Hurry! There's no time," Ernesto responded. With MJ at the helm, Ernesto grabbed the emergency brake with both hands and yanked it as hard as he could. Everyone lurched forward as the boat stopped suddenly. "Now, to get Groucho Gary off our tail, once and for all…" said Ernesto.

Eddie and MJ closed their eyes, bracing for a crash as Gary's boat sped toward them. In a flash, Ernesto dropped a large plank of wood from the back of his boat. Acting like a ramp, the plank of wood sent Groucho Gary's boat sailing nearly straight up into the air before it finally landed way off in the distance and sputtered to a stop.

"That was amazing, Ernesto!" said MJ. She handed Ernesto his corn, which looked a little smooshed after she'd been holding on to it for dear life!

"They don't call me El Capitan for nothin'," Ernesto replied, and took a bite out of his corn. "We need to get you off this boat now," he continued. "Throw me that rope!"

Rosa passed the captain a length of thick rope, which he tied into a **lasso**. With a great big heave, Ernesto threw the rope, latching it around a large rock, and pulled the boat up next to a small patch of land. "You must get off here, amigos!" he said.

"The Island of the Dolls. The old legend says that a little girl got lost on this island. A man searched and searched for many weeks trying to find her," he said with a frown on his face. "But all he could ever find was her toy rag doll. To keep that first doll company, he started collecting others, arranging them here on this island."

I'm not so sure about this, MJ thought to herself as she stepped off the boat.

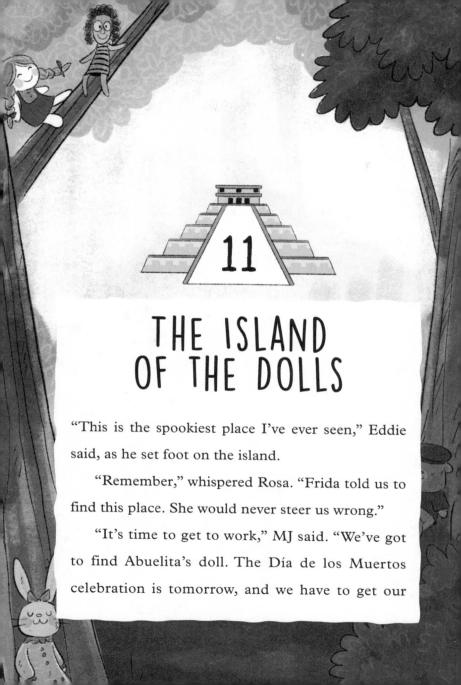

11

THE ISLAND OF THE DOLLS

"This is the spookiest place I've ever seen," Eddie said, as he set foot on the island.

"Remember," whispered Rosa. "Frida told us to find this place. She would never steer us wrong."

"It's time to get to work," MJ said. "We've got to find Abuelita's doll. The Día de los Muertos celebration is tomorrow, and we have to get our hands on the molé recipe before Groucho Gary does!"

"Groucho Gary won't be getting anything," said Eddie, pulling up the collar of his long detective's trench coat.

"Now, which of these dolls could be Abuelita's? There are hundreds of them!" MJ said.

Everywhere they looked, there were dolls, dolls, and more dolls. MJ found a cute one in a princess outfit. She picked it up off the dirt path. "Maybe this was Abuelita's favorite doll," she said. "I sure would've loved this one when I was little!"

Rosa squinted her eyes, looking carefully at the doll in MJ's hands.

"No! It has to be that one," Eddie figured, pointing at a large doll hanging from the tree to their left. "Don't you think Abuelita would've wanted a gigantic cowboy doll?"

Before Rosa could reply, the three friends heard a rustling from the bushes. Without warning, Groucho Gary appeared, clutching another doll in his greasy hands. "I've got it!" he roared. "While you fools were chatting away, I found the most expensive porcelain doll on the island. Obviously, this must be the one!" shouted Gary, as he ran off toward the shore. "So long, suckers!" he exclaimed.

Eddie looked up at his friends. Rosa could see tears welling up in his eyes. "We've been beaten," he said, kicking a rock in front of him.

"He's right," said MJ, looking gloomy as ever. "Groucho Gary has the doll, and soon he'll have the molé recipe too."

"Sorry, Rosa," Eddie said. "I guess we're not cut out to be gumshoes after all." Looking up, Eddie was perplexed to see Rosa standing there with a giant grin on her face.

"What is it?" asked MJ.

"Look," Rosa whispered, pointing toward the foot of a coconut tree. Sitting there, Eddie and MJ saw what had to be the oldest doll on the whole island. This one wasn't wearing a fancy princess costume. Instead, the tiny figurine had braided pigtails and was dressed in traditional Mexican clothes: a plain white dress with faded red and green stripes.

"You can't be serious?" said Eddie incredulously.

"Abuelita and her sister grew up on a farm in a small mountain village in the Mexican state of Oaxaca," said Rosa.

"*Wa-ha-ka*," repeated Eddie, remembering that the letter X can make an H sound in Mexico.

Rosa continued. "Back then, they wouldn't have had the money for a costly doll like Groucho Gary chose." Her voice became more and more determined. "Abuelita's doll would have to be the most simple doll on the Island of the Dolls..."

MJ picked up the doll from underneath the coconut tree. "She's perfecto!"

"Except for that totally broken windup key on her back," replied Eddie. Looking down, MJ saw a brass knob on the back of the doll that had cracked in half.

"Not to worry," Eddie said. "It turns out I am a gumshoe who really does have gum on my shoe!" He took off his left sneaker and carefully peeled a piece of gum from the bottom of it. The gum looked like it had been there for at least a year!

Rosa giggled. "I knew there was a reason I hired you!" she laughed as she began fixing the sticky gum to the back of the windup doll. "Did you know that it was the ancient Aztecs who gave the world chewing gum in the first place?" she said as she molded the gum to the back of the doll.

"Why don't you do the honors, MJ?" Rosa asked, handing her the doll.

MJ slowly cranked the key on the back of the doll three times. They fell completely silent. They could hear the gears inside beginning to whir. Then, the arms and legs of the doll began to move up and down.

Suddenly, the children heard the scratchy voice of an old lady coming from inside the doll.

"What the—" Eddie blurted out.

"It's Abuelita's voice! It must be a recording she made for us!" said Rosa. They gathered around and listened carefully.

Where the jalapeños are hot,
Through the cloud forest you walk
To a statue that talks.
Children, please hurry!
You must find me before...

The recording ended abruptly before Abuelita finished.

"What in the world could Abuelita mean? **Jalapeños** are spicy everywhere," Rosa said.

"The J in jalapeño is silent, and sounds like an H," Eddie reminded himself. "Hot! Hot! Hot!" he sang while doing a silly dance.

"This is no time for messing around, Eddie!" MJ scolded as she pulled out their trusty Awesome Enchanted Book. "There!" she said, pointing to the entry for the word jalapeño in the beginning of the J section of the AEB. She cleared her throat to start reading.

"It's a pepper!" interrupted Eddie.

"We *know* that," said MJ. "But there has to be more to the story."

While they argued, Rosa studied the AEB over MJ's shoulder. "It says here that the jalapeño is a type of spicy pepper whose name means 'from Jalapa,' the town where they were first grown," she read aloud. "We had to memorize Mexico's thirty-two states in school this year," Rosa said. "Jalapa is the capital city in the state called Veracruz."

"I think it's time we cruise to Veracruz," chuckled Eddie.

"But it's not very close," replied Rosa. "It's hundreds of miles away, near the entrance to Mexico's rain forests."

MJ looked at Rosa with amazement. "I didn't know there were rain forests in…"

MJ's words were drowned out by the thunderous roar of an engine. The kids looked down toward the shore and saw their good friend Captain Ernesto. He was waving from the cockpit of a yellow seaplane— the kind that can take off right from the water!

"If you thought my boat was fast, wait until

you get a load of this puppy," Ernesto said proudly. "What are you waiting for? Get in!"

The three friends strapped themselves into Ernesto's seaplane. "To Jalapa!" Ernesto said as the plane took off into the sky.

12

THE CLOUD FOREST

The plane had been flying for a while when Ernesto turned around from the pilot's seat. "We're almost there, kids!" he shouted. "Look down, and you'll see the city of Jalapa peeking out from the rain forest that surrounds it."

Captain Ernesto began steering the yellow seaplane toward the ground as they approached Jalapa.

Suddenly, the ride got bumpy as the plane cruised through some fluffy white clouds. "Hold on tight!" he said. "These rain forests are in the mountains, so there's always lots of clouds," he said as he guided the plane down.

"The cloud forest," MJ said, remembering Abuelita's voice from inside the doll. Just as the clouds began to clear, the roar of the engine sputtered.

"Uh oh," said Eddie. "We're running out of gas!"

"Not to worry," replied Ernesto. "We'll just have to make a water landing." Rosa looked down and saw a river snaking through the cloud forest. "Hold on to your hats!" Ernesto exclaimed as he expertly guided the seaplane down to make a perfect landing onto the river below.

"You did it!" Eddie said.

"My job here is done," replied Ernesto, beaming with pride. "Now, go find Abuelita. And take these **ponchos**," he said, throwing them three raincoats. "There's a reason it's called a *rain* forest."

With that, Eddie, MJ, and Rosa jumped out of the plane and waded to the shore.

They walked through the thick jungle for hours. Suddenly, an **armadillo** crossed the jungle path and looked at them with its beady eyes.

"The word *armadillo* means 'little armored one' in Spanish," Rosa told her friends.

"Whoa!" said Eddie. "I've never seen one in real life, but they sure do look like they have a coat of armor on them."

After a while, the kids started to feel very tired. Eddie stopped and swatted a **mosquito** away that had been buzzing around him for the better part of an hour. "I need to take a break," he said, sitting down on a big old rock.

Suddenly, the ground began to shake.

"Is this an earthquake?" asked Rosa nervously.

What happened next was truly extraordinary. A colossal stone head started to rise out of the ground in front of them. The carved boulder had big round eyes and a wide nose and lips. It must have been ten feet tall! "It's an Olmec head," whispered Eddie. He had learned about the Olmecs in school. They were the ancient people who lived in Mexico thousands of years ago and left behind mysterious massive stone heads. "What's next?" he exclaimed. "Is this thing gonna start talking?!"

As though it had heard Eddie, the stone monument began to slowly move its lips and bellowed in a deep voice:

*"Before you can go, you must be a **savvy zorro!**"*

"This must be some kind of password," said MJ.

"A *savvy zorro*?" said Eddie, scrunching up his face. But MJ had already cracked open the AEB to try to get to the bottom of it.

"*Savvy* means 'smart,'" she started. "It comes from the Spanish word *saber*, which means—"

"To know something!" said Rosa, finishing MJ's sentence.

"But what about Zorro?" Eddie asked. "Isn't he that sword-fighting hero who wears a black mask?"

Eddie sure has seen a lot of old movies, MJ thought to herself.

Eddie couldn't wait any longer, and he grabbed the AEB from MJ's hands and flipped to the end of the book. "Here it is!" he shouted. "Zorro gets his name from the Spanish word for fox." Eddie repeated the two words of the clue to himself. *A savvy zorro.* Suddenly, the password came to him, and he yelled the words in the direction of the gigantic stone head.

"SMART FOX!"

They stood silently as they watched for any kind of sign that Eddie had been right. Nothing happened. But then, the ground started rumbling again as the mouth of the colossal Olmec head opened even wider than before.

"You may enter," the Olmec head said in a thunderous, low voice, and its mouth opened wide enough for the three friends to slip inside. MJ, Eddie, and Rosa looked at one another in amazement and carefully entered the gigantic mouth of the ancient stone statue.

13

PUZZLE OF THE PYRAMID

The kids crawled through a cramped, dark tunnel until they saw a glimmer of light up ahead. "The exit!" MJ said. They shuffled through the passageway. When they finally made it out into the sunlight, the trio stood, once again amazed at the sight in front of them. Rising from the clearing ahead was a vast stone pyramid.

"I thought pyramids were only found in Egypt," whispered MJ.

"The ancient people of Mexico built pyramids too," Rosa replied. "There are many still standing all over our beautiful country. This is the famous pyramid of Chichén Itzá, built by the Mayans."

The pyramid was so tall that the top of it was covered by a tuft of clouds. Unlike the ones in Egypt, Eddie noticed that there was a set of stairs running right up the center to the very top. He raced ahead and began climbing the oversized stone steps one by one.

Rosa and MJ followed behind. As they got closer to the highest point of the pyramid, MJ turned around and looked out over the cloud forest. *What a marvelous view*, she thought to herself.

"Hurry," shouted Eddie, his voice echoing from the top.

Moments later, Rosa and MJ climbed up the last stair, totally out of breath. They hadn't been able to

see it from the ground, but there was a tiny room at the top of the pyramid! "The ancient Mayans would come up here to look at the sky," Rosa figured. "They were very interested in the planets and stars. The Mayans even had their own calendar."

Looking around the room, MJ noticed a square grid containing tiles. Each tile had a different drawing etched on it. "What in the world?" she gasped.

"That's the Mayan script," replied Rosa. "It's an ancient form of writing. Each symbol translates to a sound in the English alphabet."

Eddie saw tiles filled with outlines of animals like snakes and jaguars. There were ones that looked like people too. "This is how they wrote things down?" Eddie asked.

Suddenly, a shadow appeared, and a tall man stepped out of the darkness. "It is, indeed," he said. "And you three are going to help me solve the puzzle of the pyramid that Abuelita left here."

"Groucho Gary!" Rosa gasped. "How did you—"

"If you can't beat 'em, you can always follow 'em," Gary said, moving into the light. He was breathing heavily as if he had run a long race. "And still get to the top of the pyramid first by taking the back stairs!" he wheezed.

"We're not helping you with anything!" said Eddie. "Nada. Zip. Zilch!"

"Oh, aren't you?" Gary replied. "I found Abuelita's next clue, right here," he said, holding out a scrap of paper. "Help me now, or you'll never find your old granny!"

"Listen, pal," replied Eddie. "If you don't get your mitts off that clue, you'll never get to the recipe either." The young boy squinted his eyes, focusing on the scrap of paper in Groucho Gary's hand. "So, what's it gonna be?"

Gary looked down nervously. Finally, he read the clue out loud:

> **Guacamole** is made from a
> little lizard's skin.
>
> You've got but one chance to
> see what lies within.

"Gross," MJ said. Guacamole was one of her favorite snacks. She loved to dip nacho chips into the delicious green mush. "To think I've been eating lizard skin this whole time!"

"Don't be silly," Eddie whispered. "It's got to be Abuelita's way of giving us a clue." With that, he flipped open the Awesome Enchanted Book. "Aha!" he exclaimed. "*Guacamole* comes from a word used by ancient Aztecs that means 'avocado sauce!'"

"Of course," said Rosa. "The recipe is right there in the origin of the word! Guacamole is a traditional dish made of mashed avocado mixed with chopped onion, tomatoes, and chili peppers."

MJ looked up at the wall of letter tiles. "But it could be any of those ingredients," she said. "Which one is the little lizard?"

Groucho Gary took another step towards the kids. "The clue says you only have one chance," he threatened. "Don't mess this up..."

Suddenly, a gust of wind flipped the pages of the AEB as it fell out of Eddie's hands.

MJ picked up the book and noticed an entry for the word **alligator.** "Hey!" she called out. "You're never going to believe this."

"What is it, MJ?" asked Rosa.

"The word *alligator* comes from the Spanish word *el lagarto*, which means 'lizard,'" she said.

"How could I forget?" Rosa cried. "My father calls avocados *alligator pears* because they have scaly skins like lizards!"

"Guacamole *is* made from a little lizard's skin, after all!" said MJ. "The answer to the riddle is 'avocado!'" With Rosa's help, they got to work arranging the tiles of ancient script to spell out the word. Eddie moved the O all the way to the end. "These two are the A's," Rosa said, pointing to two identical tiles that looked like anteaters. Finally, they got the entire word into place.

"A-V-O-C-A-D-O," Eddie stood back and spelled the word out as he looked up at the Mayan script.

The entire pyramid started shifting and turning. The three friends grabbed hold of one another to keep their balance. Suddenly, the top of the pyramid became covered in clouds, and no one could see anything.

"MJ, are you okay?!" asked Eddie.

"I can hear you, but I can't see you," replied MJ. "Rosa?"

"I'm here!" said their friend. "But what's going on?!"

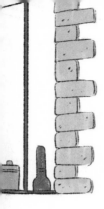

14

THE LAND OF SEVEN MOLÉS

When the clouds cleared, Eddie and MJ found that they were no longer perched atop an ancient pyramid. Instead, they were standing inside a tiny kitchen. In front of them was a huge clay pot cooking over an open fire.

"Abuelita!" they heard Rosa cry out from the other side of the kitchen.

Looking over, MJ saw an older woman with a kind, wrinkled face. Abuelita was wearing an apron and stirring the pot with a wooden spoon. *I recognize her from somewhere, but I can't put my finger on where,* MJ thought to herself.

Abuelita turned around and exclaimed, "*Dios mío!* Thank goodness! I thought you might never get here!"

"Where are we?" Eddie asked.

"Welcome to my village in the Mexican state of Oaxaca," replied Abuelita, looking down at the boy kindly. "Among many other things, the people of these mountains gave delicious molé sauce to the world!"

"Abuelita! Have you been here the whole time? We were so worried!" Rosa ran to her grandmother and gave her a big hug.

"I'm sorry to have worried you, Rosa." Abuelita squeezed Rosa tight. "Groucho Gary has been trying to steal my recipe for a long time. I caught

a glimpse of the rascal when I was waiting for my sister at the post office. When she didn't show up, I made my way here to the village. I knew you'd come looking for me, Rosa, so I left clues along the way. Now you and your friends must bring the molé back to San Miguel!

"Now I know why Oaxaca is called the Land of Seven Molés," said Rosa.

MJ looked out the kitchen window, and the view took her breath away. There were little farms dotting the rolling green mountains for miles around. MJ noticed another older woman, a few years younger than Abuelita, digging in the garden outside the kitchen.

"My sister, Maria," said Abuelita, nodding her head toward the woman outside. "She's gathering the last of the ingredients for our special molé recipe— there are twenty-four ingredients in all." Abuelita produced a long piece of paper from her apron with the full recipe.

"Wow!" the trio said at once.

Standing at the doorway with her arms over-flowing with ingredients from the garden, Abuelita's younger sister, Maria, croaked, "Once we've finished the preparations, you three must return with the molé in time for the Día de los Muertos celebration in San Miguel tonight."

Eddie, MJ, and Rosa nodded.

Without warning, a pale hand reached through the open window and snatched the treasured molé recipe right from Abuelita's hands!

"No!" MJ said. "It's that cursed Groucho Gary!"

Eddie jumped into action, darting to the door to catch the scoundrel. But, when he got there, Gary was long gone.

"The molé is mine, muchachos!" Gary's voice echoed.

Groucho Gary had the molé recipe in his clutches as he sailed off the side of the mountain in a homemade hang glider. "Game over," Eddie said dejectedly. Groucho Gary was already miles away, and there was no catching up to him now. "That bully finally got his slimy paws on the recipe."

For the first time in their whole adventure, MJ felt like she was about to cry. "What are we going to do, Rosa?" she whimpered. "Your family's restaurant…the celebration…" She trailed off as she thought about everything they were about to lose— everything Rosa's family would lose.

Rosa tried to think of something positive to say, but all that came out was a great big sigh. She sat down at the kitchen table feeling defeated.

"Ha! Ha! Ha!" cackled Maria, looking at Abuelita. The two women started laughing uncontrollably. "I can't breathe!" laughed Abuelita. She was giggling so hard that she could barely get the words out.

"Um…excuse me," said Eddie, trying to get their attention. "Maybe I'm missing something, but there doesn't seem to be anything to laugh about here. Groucho Gary won!"

"The secret ingredient!" exclaimed Abuelita.

"The likes of Groucho Gary might have *a little trouble* figuring out what it is," said Maria, finishing her sister's thought. "Still, you three ought to take this molé and get back to San Miguel as fast as you can."

Abuelita took the clay pot off the fire and fixed a red lid on top. "There!" she said as she handed the big batch of molé to Eddie and MJ.

"Aren't you coming with us, Abuelita?" Rosa asked.

"No. You are ready to carry on the tradition and bring the molé back home yourself," Abuelita said. "And so I will stay here to spend some extra time with my sister! I'll be home soon enough."

"I promise I will make you proud!" Rosa gave Abuelita a kiss on the cheek.

"You already have!" Abuelita smiled.

Taking a step closer to the old woman, MJ suddenly realized something amazing. "Mrs. Calavera?" she whispered. "You look exactly like the lady who lives at 13 Magnolia Street back home."

"Never mind that," chuckled Abuelita, winking at MJ. "There's no time to waste. Take the shortcut down the mountain through the magical garden if you want to get back to San Miguel in time!"

DÍA DE LOS MUERTOS

Eddie and MJ hiked down the mountain alongside Rosa. They took turns carrying the heavy pot of molé. When they reached the foot of the mountain, MJ saw a strange concrete archway shooting up from the middle of the jungle. "That doesn't look like it belongs here," MJ said.

"Las Pozas," Rosa whispered. "It's the magical garden that Abuelita and Maria told us about. The story goes that an artist from America named Edward James created this wonderful garden with its weird structures that look like they're straight out of a storybook!"

They stepped through the crumbling old gateway, and before they could stop themselves, Eddie, MJ, and Rosa were tumbling through the gate and down a waterfall, toward a glimmering pool of water. MJ closed her eyes and held on tight to the

molé, crouching into a cannonball position as she and her friends splashed into the pond below.

MJ's eyes were still shut tight, but her clothes weren't wet. Listening to the sounds around her, MJ figured they couldn't be in the jungle anymore. The sounds of tropical birds had been replaced by a marching band trumpeting loudly. Finally, she opened her eyes. Eddie, MJ, and Rosa, along with their big pot of Abuelita's molé, had been magically transported back to the graveyard in San Miguel, Rosa's hometown. It was nighttime, and all the townspeople were gathered for the Día de los Muertos celebration. A parade was snaking through the cemetery. All around, they noticed kids and grown-ups dressed in traditional Mexican clothes with their faces painted like skeletons.

At the far end of the graveyard, Eddie saw a line of people forming in front of a fancy-looking food truck. "Groucho Gary's Barbecue," he said, reading a hot pink neon sign.

"Come get your molé!" shouted Gary, his lanky body hanging out of the truck's window.

"We're too late," said Rosa pointing at a beat-up old table across from Groucho Gary's. Her father, Nacho, stood by with a worried look on his face, no molé in sight.

As the three made their way through the crowd, they could hear people gossiping.

"Did you hear? La Familia isn't making their world-famous molé anymore!" said a young woman.

"I guess we'll have to line up over at Groucho Gary's," replied another.

But by the time Eddie and MJ reached Rosa's father, the crowds were saying something else entirely!

"Gary's molé tastes like chalk!" exclaimed an old man.

"I want my money back," said a young boy in a skeleton costume.

Groucho Gary's face was dripping with sweat as people began lining up asking for a refund. Others were telling their friends not to buy Gary's molé at all!

Rosa's eyes widened. "Quick," she said to her father, handing him the large pot of molé. "We don't have a second to lose."

Nacho threw the pot onto his little gas stove to warm it up. "Get your molé here!" he exclaimed. "The original molé, cooked by La Familia for one hundred days!"

"The one and only family recipe!" Eddie joined in.

The line in front of La Familia's humble stand grew longer and longer, as Rosa helped serve up one whopping spoonful of molé after another.

"It's a **bonanza**!" MJ exclaimed as she helped at the cash register.

Nacho turned to Eddie and MJ, beaming with pride. "Amigos! Our restaurant is saved," he said. "How can I repay you for what you've done?"

"We're the ones who should be thanking you," replied MJ. "Día de los Muertos has taught us that we don't have to be sad when we think about our family and friends who have passed away."

"Yeah!" added Eddie. "We'll celebrate our loved ones who are gone by telling stories and eating their favorite foods! Like molé!"

Just then, Groucho Gary made his way to the front of La Familia's line. "I'm washed up," he cried to MJ and Eddie, pointing back at the sign hanging from his food truck that said

'Closed' in Spanish. *Cerrado*, it said in big red letters. "Whatever the secret ingredient was in Abuelita's molé recipe, I guess it made all the difference. I'm so sorry for stealing your recipe."

Nacho leaned over and whispered in Groucho Gary's ear. "The secret ingredient is *love*, amigo."

"Why don't you put your apron back on and come work for La Familia?" asked Rosa.

Her old nemesis looked up and smiled the biggest smile Eddie had ever seen. "Do you mean it?!" Gary shouted.

Rosa is the best and most kindhearted person I've ever known, MJ thought to herself. But it was time to go home. She smiled at her best friend, Eddie, and said, "Like my all-time hero, Amelia Earhart says, 'ALL OKAY!'"

Suddenly, the AEB drifted out of MJ's hands and began spinning in the air as huge clouds of smoke rose all around Eddie and MJ.

"Adios!" they heard Rosa's faraway voice say.

ALL SOULS' DAY

"Time to go home!" Eddie heard his Dad's familiar voice from the bottom of the stairs. "Pronto!" They were back in MJ's bedroom as if no time had passed at all.

"Holy guacamole," whispered Eddie. "Let's not forget to hide the Awesome Enchanted Book for our next adventure."

As MJ grabbed the AEB to return it for

safekeeping under her bed, she noticed something peculiar. "Look," she said, pointing toward the other end of the room. On the dresser was a small skeleton figurine made of sugar.

"There's a note!" shouted Eddie excitedly.

The two best friends ran over to the dresser to get a closer look. "It's from Rosa," MJ said excitedly as she read the note aloud. "She gave us this gift so we'll always remember our amazing adventures in Mexico."

A calavera for your ofrenda
from your new friend-a!
Happy Día de los Muertos!

GLOSSARY
OF WORD ORIGINS

Did you know that many of the words we use every day come from languages and cultures all over the world? The English language is truly a smorgasbord (that's a Swedish word that refers to a buffet with lots of different foods!). In every Word Travelers adventure, our heroes Eddie and Molly-Jean uncover the fascinating stories behind common words to save the day. Use this glossary to discover how the words in **bold** throughout the book made their way into the English language. Remember, these are just a few of the many words that we use from cultures across the globe. Some of these origins have had long and winding journeys—much

longer than we could share here. So if you want to learn more, you can become a Word Traveler too. And just like Eddie and MJ, be on the lookout for incredible word origins all around us!

alligator

(n.) ˈa-lə-ˌgā-tər

A large reptile that has a long body, thick skin, and sharp teeth. It comes from the Spanish word *el lagarto*, which means "lizard."

armadillo

(n.) ˌär-mə-ˈdi-(ˌ)lō

A mammal whose body is protected by hard, bony plates. Armadillos live in Central and South America and the southern United States. It comes from the Spanish word that means "little armored one."

avocado

(n.) ˌä-və-ˈkä-(ˌ)dō

A fruit with rough, dark green skin. It comes from the Aztec word *ahuacatl*. Because of their shape and bumpy green skin, some people call avocados "alligator pears."

barbecue

(n.)

A cooking method where meat and other food is grilled over an open fire. It comes from the Spanish word *barbacoa*, which means "frame for grilling meat."

barracuda

(n.) ˌber-ə-ˈkü-də

A fish that lives in warm ocean water and has a long body. Barracuda are fierce hunters with sharp

teeth. The word comes from the Spanish word *barracó*, which means "overlapping teeth."

bonanza

(n.) bə-ˈnan-zə

Something that produces very good results for someone. It comes from the Spanish word *bonanza*, which was originally used by sailors to mean a calm sea; hence, good luck!

breeze

(n.) ˈbrēz

A gentle wind. It comes from the Spanish word *briza*, which means "northeasterly wind."

buckaroo

(n.) ˌbə-kə-ˈrü

A cowboy, fellow, or person. Americans in the Old West started using the Spanish word *vaquero*, which means "cowboy," and gave it their own spin!

burrito

(n.) bə-ˈrē-(ˌ)tō

A Mexican food made of a flour tortilla stuffed with meat, cheese, beans, and other ingredients. It comes from the Spanish word *aburrito*, which means "little donkey." It uses the idea that donkeys can carry a lot on their backs—just like burritos can hold lots of ingredients inside them!

chocolate

(n.) ˈchä-k(ə-)lət

A food substance that is made from ground cacao seeds. Cacao is not sweet, but it is often used in candy and other sweet foods. It is also used in making certain kinds of sauces. It comes from the Nahuatl language used by the ancient Aztecs. The word *xocolatl* means "hot water."

guacamole

(n.) ˌgwä-kə-ˈmō-lē

A Mexican food made of mashed avocado usually mixed with chopped tomatoes and onion; It comes from a word in the Nahuatl language used by the ancient Aztecs, *ahuaca-molli*, which means "avocado sauce."

jalapeño

(n.) ˌhä-lə-ˈpā-(ˌ)nyō

A very hot Mexican pepper, named after Jalapa de Enríquez and the capital of the state of Veracruz in Mexico.

lasso

(n.) ˈla-(ˌ)sō

A long rope with a sliding loop on one end that is used to catch running animals such as cattle or horses. It comes from the Spanish word *lazo*, which means "tie" or "ribbon."

molé

(n.) ˈmō-lā

A traditional sauce originally used in Mexican cuisine. Generally, a molé sauce contains chocolate but is not necessarily sweet. Other ingredients include fruit, chili pepper, nut, and spices like black pepper or cinnamon. Many molé recipes have more than twenty ingredients!

mosquito

(n.) mə-ˈskē-(ˌ)tō

An insect that bites and sucks the blood of animals and people. The word means "little fly" in Spanish.

piñata

(n.) pēn-ˈyä-tə

A colorful decoration, often in the shape of an animal, that is filled with candies, gifts, or other small treats. It is suspended in the air, and blindfolded partygoers can try to break it open to spill the treats onto the ground. It comes from the Spanish word *piñata*, which originally meant "jug" or "pot."

plaza

(n.) ˈplä-zə

A public square or open space in the center of a town. It comes from the Spanish word *plaza*, which also means "town square."

poncho

(n.) ˈpän-(ˌ)chō

A blanket-like cloak with a hole in the center for a person's head. It comes from the Spanish word *poncho*, which means "woolen fabric."

savvy

(adj.) ˈsa-vē

Knowing something very well or being smart. It comes from the Spanish word *saber*, which means "to know."

siesta

(n.) sē-ˈe-stə

A rest or nap, especially in the afternoon. The Spanish word *siesta* comes from the Latin words *sexta hora*, which means "six hours after sunrise."

ten-gallon hat

(n.)

A large broad-brimmed hat, traditionally worn by cowboys. It comes from the Spanish phrase *tan galán*, which means "so gallant."

tornado

(n.) tȯr-ˈnā-(ˌ)dō

A storm of very strong winds that form a funnel-shaped cloud. Tornadoes can destroy everything in their path. The word comes from a combination of two Spanish words: *tronada*, which means "thunderstorm," and *tornar*, which means "to turn."

Vamoose!

(v.) və-ˈmüs

An exclamation when one must depart quickly. It comes from the Spanish word *vamos*, which means "let's go."

ABOUT THE AUTHOR

Raj Haldar must like words a lot. Under his alter ego, Lushlife, the rapper and multi-instrumentalist, he's spent close to a decade fitting words together into remarkable rhymes for fans all over the world. So it should come as no surprise that Raj's children's books are all about words too. His first picture book series, which includes *P Is for Pterodactyl*, was an instant smash with word nerds of all ages who love having fun with silent letters, homonyms, and other hilariously confusing parts of the English language. Now, with the Word Travelers series, Raj is introducing kids to the fascinating world of etymology and word origins, following his heroes, Eddie and Molly-Jean, on their globe-trotting adventures as they discover how common words came into the English language from cultures around the world.

ABOUT THE ILLUSTRATOR

Neha Rawat is a children's book illustrator from India and a grand prize winner of the SCBWI Summer Spectacular Portfolio Showcase 2020. She worked as a software engineer for five years before freelancing as an artist, creating custom illustrations, comics, and merchandise, before eventually moving to children's books. In her spare time, Neha can be found petting, booping and belly-rubbing dogs. Connect with her on Instagram @nrbstudio.in.

DEDICATION

To my daughter, Indira—

whose journey with words is

just beginning.